Written by Gaby Goldsack
Illustrated by Frank Endersby
Language consultant: Betty Root

This is a Parragon Publishing Book
First published in 2002

 PARRAGON PUBLISHING
Queen Street House
4 Queen Street
Bath BA1 1HE, UK

ISBN 0-75258-180-5

Printed in China

·Farmer Fred·
and the
County Fair

p

Farmer Fred was very excited. It was the day of the Sunnybridge County Fair.

Betty, Farmer Fred's wife, was entering the Jam-making Competition, and Farmer Fred was entering almost everything else.

"Maybe you should just enter one thing," said Betty.

"But there are so many wonderful competitions and so many prizes to win," laughed Farmer Fred. "How could I possibly choose? Right Patch?"

Patch, Farmer Fred's dog, wagged his tail. He was looking forward to the County Fair, too.

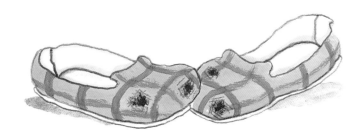

First, Farmer Fred selected his finest eggs. He carried them carefully across the yard to the vegetable patch.

"Now it's time to pick my giant pumpkin," Farmer Fred told Patch. "I've been feeding my pumpkins with my secret formula, so I'm sure to win this year."

"Bow-wow!" barked Patch, trying to warn Farmer Fred that Hattie hen was in his way.

But, WHOOAH! It was too late. Farmer Fred tripped over poor Hattie and fell headfirst into...

...the giant pumpkin. Then,

SMASH! CRACK! PLOP!

The eggs came crashing down on top of him.
Oh, what a terrible mess!

"Fiddlesticks!" said Farmer Fred. "It doesn't
look like I'll be winning the Best Eggs or Biggest
Pumpkin competitions this year. But Penny is sure
to win the Prettiest Pig Competition."

Farmer Fred and Patch made their way
across Bluebell Farm to Hog Hollow, where
Penny lived.

"Bow-wow!" barked Patch, sniffing the air.
Penny had been rolling in something very dirty—
something very dirty and
very smelly.

"Phew!" gasped Farmer Fred, as he tried to scrub Penny clean.

"Bow-wow!" barked Patch, bounding back from the farmhouse. He had brought Farmer Fred some of Betty's extra-strong laundry soap.

But it was no use. Penny was just too dirty and too smelly. They would never get her clean in time.

"Double fiddlesticks! It doesn't look like I'll be winning the prize for the Prettiest Pig this year," said Farmer Fred. "But Bonnie is sure to win the prize for the Whitest Lamb."

Farmer Fred borrowed some of Betty's best shampoo and made a bubble bath for Bonnie.

"In you go." He plunked Bonnie into the tub and began scrubbing. He closed his eyes and began to sing.

"Oh, what a beautiful morning!
Oh, what a beautiful day!
I have a wonderful feeling
I'll win some prizes today!"

"Bow-wow!" barked Patch. He tugged at Farmer Fred's sleeve.

"What is it, Patch?" asked Farmer Fred, opening his eyes.

But it was too late. Bonnie was bright pink. Farmer Fred had picked up Betty's hair dye instead of shampoo!

"Fiddlesticks!" said Farmer Fred. "It doesn't look like I'll be winning the prize for the Whitest Lamb this year. But Chloe is sure to win the prize for the Handsomest Cow."

HAIR DYE

Patch got Chloe from the pasture. Farmer Fred tied her up and found a brush.

"We'll have you gleaming in no time," said Farmer Fred. But Chloe had other ideas. As soon as the brush touched her side, she began to wriggle and squirm.

Farmer Fred had forgotten that Chloe was ticklish! Chloe would not stand still. She would never be ready in time.

"Fiddlesticks and feathers!" said Farmer Fred. "Now what am I going to do?"

"Are you ready?" shouted Betty from the farmhouse. "I don't want to be late for the Jam-making Competition."

"Double fiddlesticks and feathers!" said Farmer Fred. "I've run out of time. It doesn't look like I'll be entering any of the competitions this year."

"Bow-wow!" barked Patch jumping up and down. But Farmer Fred didn't notice.

"I just wish there was one little competition I could enter," said Farmer Fred.

Later, at the County
Fair, Betty won first
prize in the Jam-making
Competition.

Farmer Fred watched
Farmer George carry
off the prize for the Biggest Pumpkin.

"Mine was bigger than that,"
grumbled Farmer Fred.

Then he watched Farmer Dan
carry off the prize for
the Best Eggs.

"Mine were better than that,"
grumbled Farmer Fred.

Farmer Jo won the prize for the Prettiest Pig.

And Farmer Phil won the prizes for the Whitest Lamb and the Handsomest Cow.

"Bow-wow!" barked Patch, jumping up and down. But Farmer Fred didn't notice.

"Mine are better than that," grumbled Farmer Fred. "Oh, if only I could enter just one little competition."

"Bow-wow!" barked Patch. He ran around in circles pretending to round up some invisible animals.

Suddenly, Farmer Fred understood.

"Of course! The Sheepdog Competition," said Farmer Fred. "Why didn't you say something sooner, Patch?"

A few minutes later, they were in the ring. Farmer Fred whistled and Patch herded the sheep this way and that. The crowd cheered and clapped as the sheep were herded into the pen in record time.

"And the winners are Farmer Fred and Patch," said a voice over the loudspeaker.

Later, Farmer Fred showed Betty the shiny cup they had won.

"It's like I always say," said Farmer Fred happily. "It's best to concentrate on just one thing."

Betty peered over the cup she had won for her jam, and winked at Patch.